JONAH

JONAH

Dan Larsen

BARBOUR
PUBLISHING

Written by Dan Larsen. Illustrated by Ken Landgraf.

Print ISBN 978-1-61626-902-9

eBook Editions:
Adobe Digital Edition (.epub) 978-1-62029-542-7
Kindle and MobiPocket Edition (.prc) 978-1-62029-541-0

Scripture quotations identified by references are taken from the King James Version of the Bible. Other quotations in dialogue are paraphrased.

Cover design: Greg Jackson, Thinkpen Design

Published by Barbour Publishing, Inc., P.O. Box 719, Uhrichsville, Ohio 44683, www.barbourbooks.com

Our mission is to publish and distribute inspirational products offering exceptional value and biblical encouragement to the masses.

ecpa Member of the
Evangelical Christian
Publishers Association

Printed in the United States of America.
Offset Paperback Manufacturers, Dallas, PA 18612; October 2012;
D10003590

Contents

Solve the Secret Code!

At the end of each chapter, you'll find a set of numbers—it's the code to a secret message throughout the book.

Each group of four numbers stands for a single letter in the message. Your job is to pinpoint each mystery letter with the codes, then write the letters above each four-digit number group. When you've finished solving each chapter's code, read the letters from chapter one through the end of the book to find out exactly what the secret message says!

Here's how to use the codes:

- The first number is the page number—within that chapter.
- The second number is the paragraph on the page—count full paragraphs only.
- The third number is the word in the appropriate paragraph.
- The fourth number is the letter in the appropriate word—this is the letter you'll write above the number group.

Enjoy the story. . .and solving the secret message!

1
Tossed at Sea

The storm had come like a surprise attack. The only warning had been the uncanny sound of the wind. None of the mariners on board this ship had ever heard it like that before. These men had known this sea, the Mediterranean, all their lives. They made their living on it, carrying trade goods from port to port along the coast. They knew of the pleasant breezes on this sea, of going under full sail for days and nights on end. They knew, too, of the fierce storms that could blow down suddenly from the hills and mountains—thick black clouds scudding across the waters like hordes from hell.

But this. . .this was something different. Today the wind had a voice. It came at first like a howling from somewhere off in the distant, unseen mountains. But that howling was from the throat of no earthly beast! Then the howling became a wail, and the wail became a shriek. And then the force of that wind followed its voice. It whipped up the sea like a cauldron and tossed the ship like a toy.

The waves broke against the ship, drenching everyone on board. The ship plunged and reared, its timbers straining to the point of cracking. And these mariners—men who knew, and did not fear, the worst this sea had ever shown them—were afraid.

These men were from many different lands. They believed in many different gods. They cried out to those gods now, for deliverance from this storm that was not of this world. Even as they cried to their gods, they began to throw the cargo overboard to lighten the load.

The ship was foundering, each dip of its prow seeming to be its last. As the waves came over the deck, the men clung to ropes, to chains, to masts. This was not just a storm, they were sure. This was the work of some angry god, or devil.

But one man was not on deck. One man did not know, or perhaps did not care, about the fury poured out on that ship. He was down below, curled up among bundles of cloths—asleep. The expression on the sleeper's face was. . .what? Not contentment, surely. Not mere exhaustion, even. No, there was something troubled in that face, even in sleep. If the man dreamed just then, his dreams were not a comfort to him.

Up above, the shipmaster clung to the bulwark with both hands as yet another wave broke over the deck. He had given up calling out orders—there was noth-ing any of them could do now, except pray. But pray to which god? Which of the many gods these men served was now trying to destroy them? Was there some other whom no one had called upon yet? Who, or what. . .? Suddenly the shipmaster remembered. The man below. Was he there still? The shipmaster scanned the faces of the men on deck. No, that one was not there. Could he be sleeping yet, through all this?

Just then the shipmaster's heart quaked with a new fear. Could the man below be. . . ? Was he a man at all, or. . . ? No! The shipmaster shook his head and steeled his jaw. He would go below and see for himself. At the very least, the sleeping man must be made to know of his peril. And perhaps he. . . . Again, the shipmaster shook his head. He would not, he could not, fear the worst. Nor would he allow himself a false hope. But he must get to the man below!

The ship was plunging again, down, down, its prow spearing through the wall of seawater that stood up above the deck. Was this the last plunge? No, the prow came up again, the water washing over the deck. At any moment the ship would be almost level—only for a moment. Now! The shipmaster lunged for the hold.

The sleeping man awoke with a gasp. His dream had been no dream at all, then. Something did have him in its grip, was shaking him and laughing—a hideous laugh. So this was death! But, after all, he knew it would be so. He had chosen this, had he not? But wait! What was this?

"What do you mean by this, sleeper?" The voice was a man's. The hands that shook the sleeper were a man's, too.

"Get up!" came the voice again. "Call on your god, if it might be that he will think of us. We are all going to die!"

The sleeper was awake now. He saw the shipmaster above him, calling him. He felt the rising and plunging of the ship. And outside— the wailing voices of thousands of demons?

"A storm!" the shipmaster shouted. "An evil storm. . .a devil. . .the doom of us all! Why are you down here all alone? All the others are above, crying out to their gods. Come up quickly. It may be that you, too, have a god you can call on."

They went up together and came out on deck just as the ship was righting itself after a plunge. The crew were all clustered around the mainmast. They all stared now at the shipmaster and the sleeper. Now one of the crew motioned for the two men to join them. When they were all huddled together, the man who had motioned shouted, "Come, let us draw lots, that we may know who is to blame for this evil upon us."

The shipmaster nodded grimly. The sleeper bowed his head.

The name they drew was "Jonah." Every man now looked at the one whose head was bowed.

"You are Jonah?" they said.

"I am," he said.

"Tell us, we pray, who is to blame for this."

"I am."

"What do you do? Where do you come from? Of what people are you?"

The man called Jonah answered:

"I am a Hebrew, and I fear the Lord, the God of heaven, who made the sea and the dry land."

Then, with his head still bowed, he went on. Even though he served the God he had just spoken of, had served and worshipped him all his life, he was now running from him, trying to escape.

"Escape!" the men cried. "Why?"

"Because," Jonah said, "this time I cannot

obey. I can only fear. And so I have chosen to flee from my God, my Lord, rather than to obey. I have chosen, even, to die if I cannot escape."

And, so it seemed, he would not escape after all.

Now the mariners were really afraid. So there was a God who had done this, just as they thought—the God of the Hebrew man called Jonah. And this God was angry with His servant!

"Will we all die now?" they asked Jonah. And they said, among themselves, "What kind of God is this that he serves?" At the least, they were certain, He was a God to be feared.

"What must we do with you," they asked Jonah, "that your God might spare us?"

Then Jonah looked up at them. There was no fear in those eyes! And there was no tremor in the voice that said, "Take me and throw me into the sea, and it will be calm for you. It is because of me that this storm has come upon you."

The men could only stare. There was something frightening about this strange man, Jonah, the way he stood there before them, calmly and deliberately telling them to throw him overboard! Yet what else was there about him? An authority, in his face, in his voice.

These men were pagans. They knew, or

thought they knew, many gods. They did not know the one God, the Lord this man Jonah spoke of. But they did not doubt that their lives were in this Lord's hands just now. They believed that Jonah was telling the truth, that he was to blame for this storm sent by this God. Yet they were not men without human feeling. Not one of them had any desire to throw a living man overboard at sea. Instead, a new desperation, a new determination, rose up among them. They swarmed below and strapped themselves to the rowing benches.

"To shore!" they cried. "To shore or die!"

But the ship would not obey the mariner's oars. It just plunged and rose on the waves, and its timbers began to splinter. The men could row no more.

Jonah was still above, clinging to the mainmast. The men came up to him, their eyes downcast. Jonah struggled to his feet. "You must take me," he said, "and cast me into the sea. It must be so—my life for yours. Cast me

14

over or perish, one and all."

Then they cried out to Jonah's God:

"We beg You, O Lord, do not let us die for this man's life. Do not lay innocent blood upon us—for You, O Lord, have done this as You pleased."

And they threw Jonah overboard.

The frothy waves seemed to open jaws and swallow the man whole. Instantly the screaming winds—like myriad birds of prey—lifted from the sea and shrieked off into the sky. The next moment there was silence. The sea was calm.

And the mariners stood in awe on the now-gently rolling deck of their ship. And one by one they took from their pockets their little idols, the carved bone or wooden images of their gods, and threw them into the sea. And the men made vows, one to another. They would fear this God now and forever, they swore, this one true God—whose servant they had just sent to the bottom of the sea!

Secret Code:

<u>   </u> <u>   </u> <u>   </u> <u>   </u> <u>   </u>
3-2-4-3   5-3-4-2 6-2-3-3 4-2-4-2 6-3-3-5

<u>   </u> <u>   </u> <u>   </u> <u>   </u> <u>   </u>
2-2-6-4 7-5-3-3 1-1-3-2 7-5-5-1 2-1-2-4 5-2-4-2

2
The Call

There was darkness. Total darkness. And something wet, dense, holding him in a soft, cocoon-like embrace. There was movement past him, a slow, rhythmic pulsing. He could breathe, though the air—if such it could be called—was thick, warm, and oily.

They had thrown him overboard, at his

urging. He had felt the shock of the cold sea-water as his body struck the waves. And then something else, something horrible. As he plunged down and down into the black depths, the sea seemed to form itself into a giant maw, to rush up at him and gulp him down headfirst.

And the sea—or something—held him like that, in this place where there was no light, no sound, no freedom of movement—and where, it seemed to Jonah, there was no time. Was this death, then? Was this what he had asked for? If this was separation from God, then this was death. And here, Jonah felt, God was not. Jonah was alone. It would be too late now, he realized with a horror, to pray for death—too late for anything, but this!

But in this place, this tomb of eternal night and terror, Jonah began to remember.

There was his home, a place called Gath-hepher, in the land of Samaria. There was his father, whose name was Amittai. Jonah's people were of the ten tribes of Israel that had settled in Samaria. From the time he was old enough to understand, Jonah knew the stories, of their father Abraham, of Israel's captivity in the land of Egypt, of Moses and of Israel's deliverance from Egypt, of the land God promised to Israel.

He knew of Israel's first king, David, and David's son Solomon, and Solomon's son Rehoboam. It was during the reign of Rehoboam that Israel was divided, the tribes of Judah and Benjamin remaining in the cities of Judah, and the other ten tribes spreading out into the land of Samaria.

Jonah knew, too, that he was different. For as long as he could remember, he had felt that way. Others did not understand him. Often he did not understand himself. As a boy he learned that others did not see things he saw, did not feel things he felt. At times he felt he was watching the people and the things of his world through eyes that were not his own, eyes that somehow not only saw, but, in seeing, also heard and felt and, most of all, understood. There were yearnings in Jonah's heart that, for a time, he did not understand. Sometimes they frightened him. Often when his heart was stirred so, he would go off by himself, into the hills or out into the desert.

His name, he had been told, meant "dove." Sometimes he felt his heart to be like a dove, taking wing he knew not where—and he must follow, to find the place where it lighted. ("And I said, Oh that I had wings like a dove! for then

would I fly away, and be at rest"—Psalm 55:6.)
In his wanderings, seeking the resting places of
his heart, Jonah often felt that he was not alone.
Like the dove, its wings gently pattering against
the window of his soul. . .a voice was calling
him.

And then one day Jonah found the resting
place of his heart. The Dove had alit in his soul.
Then Jonah understood, the Dove was a Spirit,
the Spirit was a Word, and the Word now had a
new voice—Jonah's.

Then Jonah knew he had the same Spirit
of the great prophets of God, Elijah and Elisha,
who had lived just before Jonah's time. The secret to the prophet's power, Jonah understood
at last, was an opened window to his soul. The
Dove could go in and out as He chose. And the
prophet's heart—every beat of it, every drop of
blood in it—belonged to the Lord, the Living
God.

Jonah was such as this. He loved the Lord
with all his heart, all his mind. He would talk
with the Lord, share his deepest feelings with
the Lord, his closest friend, his beloved brother,
as well as his Master. The Lord, too, would
whisper His secrets to Jonah and share His
heart. Like the prophets Elijah and Elisha,

Jonah could speak for the Lord, because he knew the One whose Voice, whose Word, had found a resting place in Jonah's heart. . . .

Jonah's deep-sea tomb seemed to shudder. Something like weeds or giant fingers squeezed him and then released him, squeezed and released. Suddenly his memories were gone, and the icy terror of this place gripped his heart again. He was weak. His breaths came slowly, painfully. His skin burned. And constantly something was moving around him, swimming past him, or crawling over him. The horror, the panic, that closed over his heart was so real that he could feel its talons, and the pain sent spasms up to his throat. Suddenly he could not breathe at all. He felt his mind going blank, his body growing numb. . . .

He remembered the call. The word of the Lord had come, as it had come many times before. But this one. . . this one was so different: Get up, go to Nineveh, that great city, and speak against it, for their wickedness cries out against them to Me.

To Nineveh! To the heathen! That great, evil city in the kingdom of Assyria! And the Lord God. . .a God of mercy. . .to speak a warning to the heathen. . .to use His own holy name among them. . . . Did God Himself wish to blacken His own name among the heathen? Jonah's heart belonged to his God. But this word. . .so confusing, so frightening. Was it God's testing of Jonah's heart, of his devotion?

Many times in the past, he knew, the Lord would speak to His own people, through one of His servants such as Jonah. And whenever God's people listened to the word of the prophet and repented, God would spare them the punishment He had warned them of. Now what if God warned Nineveh of its destruction? Could they, like God's own people Israel, heed the warning and repent? Would God spare them? Then all the world—the enemies of God and of God's people—would know, and would tell their children forever, that God's word did not come true!

At this command, "Go to Nineveh," Jonah's heart failed him. He could not. Though all the world be a liar, let God be true! Then Jonah was afraid. He tried to run, to flee from the place where he had known his God, where the Lord had spoken to Jonah so many times.

He found a ship bound for Tarsus in Cilicia, a land outside of Samaria. Jonah would cut himself off from God's people, would separate himself from God, even, rather than be the one to mock the name of God in the earth.

But then that awful storm, the hand of God against that ship at sea. And Jonah knew he could not escape. And now there was only this, this dark, terrible place that was—that must be—worse by far than death.

Secret Code:

$$\overline{\rule{1.2em}{0pt}}\ \overline{\rule{1.6em}{0pt}}\ \overline{\rule{1.6em}{0pt}}\ \overline{\rule{1.2em}{0pt}},$$

2-3-1-1 4-1-2-2 6-3-6-4 7-1-1-2 ,

1-2-3-4 3-2-6-3 5-1-1-2 6-2-9-3 2-1-6-4 ,

3
On Dry Ground

There was light, somewhere. There had been no light at all, but it was there now, however tiny a flame it seemed. And Jonah, in his dark night of death, looked toward that light like. . .like a dove homing to its resting place. The Spirit of the Lord was there now, in the depths, like a beacon on a faraway shore. And Jonah saw. Now, more than ever before, he saw that his place, the resting place of his heart, was with the Spirit of the Lord. Come success or failure, health or sickness, life or death—he could never again try to separate himself from his Lord and God.

Then Jonah prayed to God:

And said, I cried by reason of mine affliction unto the LORD, and he heard me; out of the belly of hell cried I, and thou heardest my voice.

For thou hadst cast me into the deep, in the midst of the seas; and the floods compassed me about: all thy billows and thy waves passed over me.

Then I said, I am cast out of thy sight; yet I will look again toward thy holy temple.

The waters compassed me about, even to the soul: the depth closed me round about, the weeds were wrapped about my head.

I went down to the bottoms of the mountains; the earth with her bars was about me for ever: yet hast thou brought up my life from corruption, O LORD my God.

When my soul fainted within me I remembered the LORD: and my prayer came in unto thee, into thine holy temple.

They that observe lying vanities

forsake their own mercy.
But I will sacrifice unto thee with
the voice of thanksgiving; I will pay
that that I have vowed. Salvation is
of the LORD.

JONAH 2:2–9

What was this? Something was happening, some new movement. There was still that pulsating movement all around him, but now it seemed that the sea itself was rushing downward past him. What new terror was this? His heart was beating wildly. But. . .was the light growing brighter?

Then suddenly his body was squeezed so tightly that he could not breathe. And he felt himself being thrust up, up, up. . . .

The light was blinding. And something was in his face, stinging his eyes. He gasped for breath—and then sputtered and coughed. The taste was bitter, like salt. No, something was not in his face; his face was in. . .seawater!

He raised his head. The light was like daggers in his eyes. He shut them tightly again. Was he in the sea? He should swim, then, he thought. He tried, but his arms and legs would not obey. The saltwater was in his face again.

And he tasted something else.

Sand! He was on the beach! Weakly, slowly, he crawled up out of the shallow water lapping the shore. Then he collapsed.

He slept. The hours passed, the tide came in. The cold seawater on Jonah's legs woke him. The sun was low in the sky. Jonah felt much stronger, though his arms and legs were still shaky. He crawled up the beach 'til he could go no farther. He sat there, his heart pounding from the exertion. Then, with a horror, he noticed his skin. It was stark white and shriveled like a dried fig. And what was that terrible odor? A nauseous, oily, fishy. . .a fish! Jonah smelled like a fish!

Only then did he realize what had happened to him. He had been in the belly of a great fish! It must be so. How long? He did not know. But that would be the only way he could have remained alive, all the while breathing, under the sea. So the stories and legends must be true. Sailors had passed these tales down for generations, of fish of immense size in this sea. One account told of a fisherman having fallen overboard and been swallowed by a fish the size of a fishing boat. A quick-thinking sailor had harpooned the fish, which then vomited out the fisherman—whole and well! Another story had it that a fish the size of a whale had washed up onto shore, dead. On cutting the fish open, fishermen found the body of a horse in the fish's stomach.

So God had prepared such a fish to swallow Jonah whole. Jonah had no doubt of this. As he sat there, watching the tide wash up over the beach and the sun go down over the sea, Jonah's heart was filled with worship. His spirit welled up with praise, as did the psalmist's long before:

O LORD my God, I cried unto thee, and
thou hast healed me.
O LORD, thou hast brought up my
soul from the grave: thou hast kept me
alive, that I should not go down to the pit.
Sing unto the LORD, O ye
saints of his, and give thanks at the
remembrance of his holiness.
For his anger endureth but a

moment; in his favour is life: weeping
may endure for a night, but joy cometh
in the morning.

PSALM 30:2–5

Bless the LORD, O my soul. O LORD
my God, thou art very great; thou art
clothed with honour and majesty.

PSALM 104:1

The LORD reigneth, he is clothed with
majesty; the LORD is clothed with
strength, wherewith he hath girded
himself: the world also is stablished,
that it cannot be moved.

Thy throne is established of old:
thou art from everlasting.

The floods have lifted up, O LORD,
the floods have lifted up their voice; the
floods lift up their waves.

The LORD on high is mightier than
the noise of many waters, yea, than the
mighty waves of the sea.

Thy testimonies are very sure:
holiness becometh thine house, O
LORD, for ever.

PSALM 93

Jonah's heart was now silent. The sun had dropped below the horizon over the sea. The twilight was still. The waves lapped the shore in a melancholy rhythm.

And then, deep within Jonah's spirit, the voice came again, as clearly as the first time: Go to Nineveh.

Secret Code:

‾‾‾‾ ‾‾‾‾ ‾‾‾‾ ‾‾‾‾ ‾‾‾‾
1-1-6-2 3-1-4-3 2-1-2-2 4-1-1-3 5-1-2-1

‾‾‾‾ ‾‾‾‾ ‾‾‾‾
7-1-2-5 1-1-3-4 3-4-1-2

‾‾‾‾ ‾‾‾‾ ‾‾‾‾ ‾‾‾‾ ‾‾‾‾ ‾‾‾‾ :
4-2-2-4 5-1-4-3 4-3-1-1 2-1-3-1 3-3-2-1 4-2-1-2

4
Abner

The dusty road was deserted but for one traveler, a short, roundish man with a bright sash around his robe and a white turban. His clothes, and the camel he was leading—laden with bundles of cloths and baskets and strings of beads—marked him for a merchant. He walked slowly, humming badly out of tune. As he came to a small tree by the side of the road, he stopped. He had not noticed the man sitting there in the shade.

"Greetings, stranger, and God's blessings upon you," the merchant said, bowing.

At this the man under the tree looked up—

and the merchant's breath caught with a gasp. The face that looked at him was like death! The skin was pale—no, not pale, but bleached white. The eyes stared out of hollow sockets, the cheeks were sunken. And...what was that horrible smell?

"Do not be alarmed," the man under the tree said. "I am not a ghost, though perhaps I appear as one to you." He gestured to the ground beside him. "You may join me here if you like—if you dare."

"Th–thank you," the merchant stammered. Then, resisting the impulse to continue staring, he bowed again. "I am Abner of Joppa. I am indeed weary of my journey and in need of rest. Thank you, kind sir. I will join you." He looked up again. "Er, may I, ah, offer you some refreshment? Is there something...?" He bowed again. "Whatever you wish. I am your servant."

He sat down, not too close but with as pleasant a smile as he could manage.

The stranger said, "You are being brave, I know. I am not a ghoul, nor am I a pirate or a convict. I am a Hebrew, a servant of the one true God, the God of Israel and Judah. My name is Jonah. I was alive, and then I was dead. And now I am alive again."

The man called Abner gasped again.

Jonah looked at him. "If you like, I will tell you. It is a long tale, and. . .and I am not proud to tell it." He was looking directly into the other man's eyes.

"Sir, you honor me," Abner said. "I am your most humble servant." He held up his hand. "But first, if you will indulge my vanity, I would consider it a privilege to. . . ." He scrambled to his feet and began ruffling through a wicker basket on his camel. "Ah, here!" he said, "and, yes, this! and this, and, mmmm, yes, this!" He came over to Jonah with new bright-colored clothes draped over his arms.

"My friend, I see with my own eyes that you have had some sore adventure. Please allow me to serve you thus." He held out his arms with the clothes, smiling. "And I have water, and ointment, and food. Please, bathe and dress yourself and take something to eat."

"I think that, at least for now, I am better as I am," said Jonah.

The merchant's face fell. His arms slowly sank to his sides. "I do not offer this as a merchant," he said, "but as a brother and a fellow servant of the Lord God. I, too, am an Israelite, and I, too, fear, and serve, the living God."

A deep light flashed in Jonah's eyes. "Then you will understand when I tell you my story. I thank you for your kindness. For now, though, I think I will just take a little food, and. . .I am very thirsty. Perhaps some water?"

Abner quickly stuffed the clothes back into the basket, rummaged in another basket, and brought a new bundle over to Jonah. He spread out a cloth on the ground and laid out a flask of water and handfuls of figs and dates and small barley cakes. "Now, please, refresh yourself," he said. He sat down. "And pray do not hurry. Whenever you will, please tell me of your adventure. I am your servant." He bowed his face to the ground.

"Tell me," Jonah said, "how many days have passed since the last Sabbath?"

"Ah, let me see. . . ." Abner spread out his fingers and studied his hand. "Four," he said.

"Then, to begin with, I have been three days and nights in the belly of a fish."

The merchant Abner listened in awe as the prophet told his story. The sun dropped lower and lower in the sky as Jonah told of his special appointment by God to the office of prophet among the people of Israel. He told of the times and ways the Lord had spoken to him, of how Jonah had in turn spoken the Lord's word, and of how God was always faithful to His word.

"I know this!" Abner said. His face was beaming. "God is always faithful to His word."

Jonah went on, telling of his latest call, to speak against Nineveh. He told of his fear, his disobedience, his attempt to flee from the land of God's people, where Jonah had known the Lord, known Him, feared Him, loved Him with all His heart and soul and might, had spoken with Him, heard His voice, and—until this time—obeyed Him.

Then came the night terror in the deep, his living burial in the sea. Then his salvation and, again, the Lord's command to go to Nineveh.

Jonah was now silent. The sun was just sinking below the distant hills. The two men sat without speaking. A low evening breeze had begun to move in the branches of the tree, and the leaves spoke now in hushed whisperings.

Jonah sighed. "I

am weary," he said. "I am so very weary." He lay down and curled up on the ground.

Abner sat still for several minutes, his head bowed, his eyes shut. Then, as though startled from sleep, he got up and bustled over to his camel. He took a blanket from the bundles and gently spread it over the sleeping man. The little merchant took out another blanket for himself and wrapped it about his shoulders. He, too, had journeyed long today and was tired. But he did not lie down, not just yet. He sat on the ground under the whispering tree. He wanted to think.

Nineveh! Abner shuddered. That proud, evil place, a city as large as an entire country! In the very heart of Assyria, an empire as evil as the night is dark. An empire where kings not only were the cruelest the world had ever known, but also boasted of their cruelty and taunted the Lord God Almighty. And this prophet Jonah? Abner looked at the sleeping form. Sent by God to preach to the Ninevites? To warn them of their doom? The Lord God giving warning to the heathen, the children of the devil!

But this man Jonah was a true man of God, Abner was sure. There was something about the calm, unhurried way he spoke, the sureness of his voice. But, no, these were not all. Abner's brow was creased in thought. Not just the words the man spoke, not just his face—there was no guile in that face! Not just, oh, not even those eyes! Eyes that seemed to pierce Abner's own, seemed to see right into, even through, his very soul. No, there was something more!

It was something in Abner himself, he suddenly realized. Something in him, in his own heart, that responded to the prophet's words, something in his breast that seemed to leap up, to cry out, "Hear this! Hear this! Here is truth! Here is life!" His own heart, Abner realized, had absorbed the truth of the prophet's words—like a "dry and thirsty land, where no water is" (Psalm 63:1).

Then Abner suddenly decided something. The dry and thirsty land that was his own heart wanted more of this water. He had listened, just now, to a man of God speaking words of truth. He wanted to hear more.

Nineveh was a long, long way away,

probably thirty days. Maybe he would go with this prophet, part of the way, anyhow. Yes, maybe he would.

The merchant sat there for a long while, listening to the leaves overhead, to the prophet's steady breathing, to the far-off night sounds, and to his own heart beating. Finally he laid himself down and went to sleep.

But his dreams that night were troubled ones.

Secret Code:

$\overline{\text{2-1-4-1}}$ $\overline{\text{6-1-1-3}}$ $\overline{\text{8-2-3-1}}$ $\overline{\text{3-2-5-1}}$

$\overline{\text{4-5-4-1}}$ $\overline{\text{5-1-1-1}}$ $\overline{\text{7-3-3-7}}$ $\overline{\text{1-2-5-2}}$

5
Journey to Nineveh

They would have to go north to Damascus in Syria, about six days, Abner said. As a merchant he had traveled the familiar caravan routes across the Syrian Desert. He had been to Babylon in the south, and as far east as Mari on the Euphrates River. But he had never gone beyond, to Mesopotamia or—God forbid—to Assyria.

How far would he go with this prophet Jonah? Abner wondered. Well, he would decide later. They had a long way to go.

At Abner's urging, Jonah had bathed and put on the new clothes Abner gave him. This pleased the kind-hearted merchant very much.

They would try to join up with some caravan going east if they could, Abner told Jonah. Traveling across the desert was much safer that way.

Two days into their journey north, at midday, the two men were sitting in the shade of a small tent that Abner always carried. Desert travelers rested during the hottest part of the day, taking up their journey again in the cooler late afternoon and early evening. Sometimes caravans traveled at night, when the way was clear enough, and especially when there was light from the moon.

The man Jonah did not talk much. During the two days of their journey, Jonah spoke only to answer the other's questions, which were not many—the little merchant was not quite sure he dared ask too many questions of this strange, silent prophet.

Now Jonah sat as still as a carved figure, seemingly absorbed in his thoughts. Abner, his eyes downward and his mouth set firmly, was determined to respect the other's silence.

But then the prophet, without moving or looking up, said, "What is it you wish to ask me?"

Abner took a sharp breath. "I. . .I. . ."

The other looked up. He looked directly into the merchant's eyes.

Abner, as if in a trance, said, "Tell me about the kingdom of Assyria."

Jonah was silent for what seemed like a very long time to Abner. The prophet's eyes were still fixed on the merchant's, but now, Abner thought, the prophet was not staring at him, did not even know he was there. He was. . .looking. . .or was he looking at all? Suddenly the merchant felt a shudder pass over him, starting at the top of his head and rippling down to his very toes. There was no sound from the desert, no breeze on the flap of the tent doorway, not even the sound of his own heartbeat—but this stillness was like the noise of brass gongs compared with the deep hush that just now came into the tent. And the prophet, the seer, closed his eyes. . .and saw.

They called themselves "The People of Asshur"—Assyrians. Asshur was their god. They named the greatest city of their empire after him. Their kings were, they believed, the agents of Asshur.

And they worshipped Ishtar, the goddess of fertility and war. They called her the Lady of Heaven, the Queen of Heaven. She was known by other names, too: Ashtoreth. Astarte.

The Assyrians worshipped this god and this goddess. They built temples for them, they sacrificed people to them, and in their honor they spread terror and panic throughout their vast empire for more than seven centuries. Their

armies had chariots and bowmen, slingers and spearmen, ramps and battering rams. They bathed their war goddess in blood, they boasted. Fresh blood was her choice wine, her best ointment, they said. And she drank and was yet thirsty, she bathed and would not be refreshed, she anointed herself and would not be soothed.

No, this blood-bathed goddess, this "Queen of Heaven," would not be contented. She would reach out to divide forever and, if she could, to devour the twelve tribes of Israel, the chosen people of the Most High God.

> *The children of Israel did evil in the sight of the LORD, and served Baalim: And they forsook the LORD God of their fathers, which brought them out of the land of Egypt, and followed other gods, of the gods of the people that were round about them, and bowed themselves unto them, and provoked the LORD to anger. And they forsook the LORD, and served Baal and Ashtaroth.*
>
> JUDGES 2:11–13

Then Solomon, the son of Israel's first king, David, would bring God's wrath on Israel, which would be divided into the land of Judah in the south and Samaria in the north. Solomon married many women from foreign lands. They caused him to turn away from God and worship other gods. He built temples for the gods Chemosh and Ammon, and to the goddess Astarte. He did this even though God appeared to him twice and commanded him not to worship foreign gods.

The LORD said unto Solomon, Forasmuch as this is done of thee, and thou hast not kept my covenant and my statutes, which I have commanded thee, I will surely rend the kingdom from thee, and will give it to thy servant.

1 KINGS 11:11

Because that they have forsaken me, and have worshipped Ashtoreth the goddess of the Zidonians, Chemosh the god of the Moabites, and Milcom the god of the children of Ammon, and have not walked in my ways, to do that which is right in mine eyes, and to keep my statutes and my judgments, as did David his father. Howbeit I will not take the whole kingdom out of his hand: but I will make him prince all the days of his life for David my servant's sake, whom I chose, because he kept my commandments and my statutes

1 KINGS 11:33–34

It was under Rehoboam, Solomon's son, that this word of the Lord to Solomon came to pass.

And Rehoboam went to Shechem: for all Israel were come to Shechem to make him king. And it came to pass, when Jeroboam the son of Nebat, who was yet in Egypt, heard of it, (for he was fled from the presence of king Solomon, and Jeroboam dwelt in Egypt;) That they sent and called him. And Jeroboam and all the congregation of Israel came, and spake unto Rehoboam, saying, Thy father made our yoke grievous: now therefore make thou the grievous service of thy father,

and his heavy yoke which he put upon us, lighter, and we will serve thee. . . . And the king answered the people roughly, and forsook the old men's counsel that they gave

him; And spake to them after the
counsel of the young men, saying, My
father made your yoke heavy, and
I will add to your yoke: my father
also chastised you with whips, but I
will chastise you with scorpions. . . .
So when all Israel saw that the king
hearkened not unto them, the people
answered the king, saying, What
portion have we in David? neither have
we inheritance in the son of Jesse: to
your tents, O Israel: now see to thine
own house, David. So Israel departed
unto their tents. But as for the children
of Israel which dwelt in the cities of
Judah, Rehoboam reigned over them.
Then king Rehoboam sent Adoram,
who was over the tribute; and all Israel
stoned him with stones, that he died.
Therefore king Rehoboam made speed
to get him up to his chariot, to flee to
Jerusalem. So Israel rebelled against the
house of David unto this day.
1 KINGS 12:1–4, 13–14, 16–19

This northern kingdom would become
known as Samaria. The southern kingdom was

called Judah. Both kingdoms continued for generation after generation to sin against God by worshipping the Assyrians', and others', gods and goddesses.

They built pagan temples in all their towns. On hills and under trees they put up stone pillars and images of the goddess Astarte. The Lord sent His messengers and prophets again and again to warn Israel and Judah of their crimes against Him.

But Israel and Judah refused to listen.

"How long do you suppose the Lord will wait before He punishes Israel?" the prophet now asked the merchant in their tent by the road.

Abner said nothing. But he thought, *I do not know, but I do not wish to know!*

The prophet looked intently into the other's face. "Perhaps you do not wish to know," he said. "Nor do I. But I believe. . .I have seen. . .it will not be long, I think."

"And you think Assyria. . . ?"

Jonah nodded gravely. "It is poised there, stretched out over our lands like a giant hammer, like a foot about to crush an insect, and. . ."

"And it is where we are going!" said Abner.

Secret Code:

___ ___ ___ ___
3-2-4-1 2-1-6-2 7-1-3-2 9-1-3-3

___ ___ ___ ___ ___ ___ ___
3-1-4-4 4-1-3-3 1-1-3-2 2-5-4-2 9-2-2-2 1-1-1-3 4-2-2-3

6
Troubled Dreams

They had stayed in Damascus in Syria for three days, to rest. Abner had done some trading there and had replenished their food and water

supply for the next leg of their journey. Then it was six more days north and east along the ancient caravan route across the Syrian Desert and into Tadmor.

This was the one splash of green on all

that flat, tan expanse of desert, an oasis of palm trees that had grown up around a spring of fresh water.

Early that morning they had seen the green on the horizon, had kept on a course straight toward it as soon as it came into view. But the hours went by, the two men walked on and on, and still the green spot ahead seemed to grow no larger, seemed even to be moving, staying out of reach.

Then at dusk, great green giants seemed to loom up suddenly out of nowhere and surround the two travelers, and Jonah and Abner were within the tiny city among the trees.

The spring that gave life to this green place in the desert ran deep. It had never gone dry, in the memory of anyone living there. The two men drank their fill and bathed their faces. Abner let his camel drink, and drink, and drink, while he lay on the soft grass, his eyes closed. Jonah sat with his legs crossed and his head bowed.

Night fell quickly. Lights appeared now, one by one, as the lanterns were lit along the road that wound among the trees.

"Come," said Abner. "There is an inn here that I know of. It is a good place. There is food, and wine, and. . ."

He glanced a little uneasily at the prophet. "And they do not ask questions of strangers here."

The inn was not crowded. There were not many travelers through here, most preferring to go along the caravan route to the north that skirted the desert. As the two men sat with their food and drink, Jonah said, "I may never be able to repay you, you know, friend."

Abner looked up sharply. Before he could speak, the other said, "I left what I had on the ship when I. . .when they. . .you know."

"Ah, but. . ." The little merchant did not look happy. He cleared his throat and seemed to square his shoulders. "Sir, you must know this, it is not for any hope of profit that I am doing this. For me it is not always business. I believe I, ah, I think. . ."

"I think yours is a good heart," the prophet said.

"Mine, alas, is a heart that fears much and understands little." Abner took a long drink and then sat staring intently at his goblet for several moments.

"God will repay you, anyway," Jonah said, "even if I cannot."

"God is good. That I know. But—I wonder, how is it that you. . . ?"

"That I speak so surely of God when I am, in fact, one who disobeyed, who ran?"

Abner looked up and caught the prophet's eye. The look was one of severity, but also of humility. The merchant said, "I think, yes, that that is my question. Though I know I have no right to ask." He quickly looked down at his goblet again. Then he said, "Is it now that you do not fear, whereas before you did? Or do you go with. . .with some new vision that all will be well?" He looked at Jonah again. "You do believe this, don't you?"

The prophet looked deeply troubled. "I do not believe this," he said.

The merchant stared at Jonah.

"I do not think I believe anything just now," Jonah said.

"Then—then, why. . . ?" sputtered Abner.

"Why do I yet go to Nineveh? When my heart does not comfort me? When the Lord Himself has not promised me anything?"

Abner just nodded, still staring.

"Because the Lord God said to go," Jonah said. There was a brief flash, like a little flame, in his eyes. "I ran from the Lord at His first word. And then I was dead, or as good as dead. I was, indeed, cut off from the presence of the Lord. But then I was brought to life again. The life that I live is from the Lord—from Him alone. And whereas my old life was not able to obey this word from the Lord, this new life— His life in me—is able. I go now, not merely by my own obedience, but by the Word of God."

Before I was afflicted I went astray: but now have I kept thy word.

PSALM 119:67

For the word of the LORD is right; and all his works are done in truth.

He loveth righteousness and judgment: the earth is full of the goodness of the LORD.

By the word of the LORD were the heavens made; and all the host of them by the breath of his mouth.

He gathereth the waters of the sea together as an heap: he layeth up the depth in storehouses.

Let all the earth fear the LORD: let
all the inhabitants of the world stand in
awe of him.
     For he spake, and it was done; he
commanded, and it stood fast.
                                    PSALM 33:4–9

Abner was studying Jonah's face. For once, the merchant did not feel even a little afraid to meet the prophet's eye. Abner did not understand why this was so, but there was suddenly some new strength in him, a strength to believe. And fear, for the moment, was gone.

Jonah said, "My way is laid out for me by the Lord. And I will walk in it. As the psalmist wrote, 'Thy word is a lamp unto my feet, and a light unto my path' (Psalm 119:105). Remember, though, my friend, it is my path because it is ordered so. You are free to choose another."

Abner stared at the prophet long and hard. Finally he said, "I think I will go on with you still—for awhile."

They finished their meal in silence. The firelight played against the stone walls, ghostly shadows flitting about the large room. There were only a few other guests here tonight. Two of them sat in a darkened corner, their faces concealed in the shadow. They were silent. Had they been listening? Abner wondered. He looked cautiously about the room. His new-found courage was fleeting, it seemed. He felt his heart already growing troubled.

The innkeeper showed them up to their room. There were two beds of straw and one small window. The stable boy had earlier bedded down Abner's camel—after, of course, Abner had carried all his bundles and baskets of goods up to their room.

The two men fell asleep quickly. But this night it was Jonah's turn for troubled sleep. Did he dream of what lay ahead? Or—did he see?

Did he see, perhaps, that the foot that was Assyria would indeed come down on the insect Samaria? It would be only another one hundred years or so before Samaria would fall to the Assyrian empire. The Lord God would finally give Samaria as captives to the Queen of Heaven—because, as was their habit, they would not listen to His warnings, would not obey.

And there was another man of God, another prophet, whom God sent, once again, to warn the people of Samaria.

The LORD hath a controversy with the inhabitants of the land, because there is no truth, nor mercy, nor knowledge of God in the land. By swearing, and lying, and killing, and stealing, and committing adultery, they break out, and blood toucheth blood. Therefore shall the land mourn, and every one that dwelleth therein shall languish, with the beasts of the field, and with the fowls of heaven; yea, the fishes of the sea also shall be taken away.

HOSEA 4:1–3

I have seen an horrible thing in the house of Israel: there is the whoredom of Ephraim, Israel is defiled.

HOSEA 6:10

Set the trumpet to thy mouth. He shall come as an eagle against the house of the LORD, because they have transgressed my covenant, and trespassed against my law. Israel shall cry unto me, My God, we know thee. Israel hath cast off the thing that is good: the enemy shall pursue him. . . .

For they are gone up to Assyria, a wild
ass alone by himself: Ephraim hath
hired lovers. Yea, though they have
hired among the nations, now will I
gather them, and they shall sorrow
a little for the burden of the king of
princes.

HOSEA 8:1–3, 9–10

But through this prophet, Hosea, the Lord
would offer His people yet one more chance, and
a promise.

O Israel, return unto the LORD thy God;
for thou hast fallen by thine iniquity.
    Take with you words, and turn to
the LORD: say unto him, Take away all
iniquity, and receive us graciously: so
will we render the calves of our lips.
    Asshur shall not save us; we will
not ride upon horses: neither will we
say any more to the work of our hands,
Ye are our gods: for in thee the father-
less findeth mercy.
    I will heal their backsliding, I will
love them freely: for mine anger is
turned away from him.

I will be as the
dew unto Israel:
he shall grow as
the lily, and cast
forth his roots as
Lebanon.

His branches
shall spread, and
his beauty shall be
as the olive tree,
and his smell as Lebanon.

They that dwell under his shadow
shall return; they shall revive as the
corn, and grow as the vine: the scent
thereof shall be as the wine of Lebanon.

Ephraim shall say, What have I to
do any more with idols? I have heard
him, and observed him: I am like a
green fir tree. From me is thy fruit
found.

HOSEA 14:1–8

Did the same vision that stirred the heart
of Hosea also work in the prophet Jonah? What
did he dream tonight? What made him turn in
his bed and made his breath catch now and
again?

The Lord's warning, and promise, to His people Israel. . .in the land of Samaria. . .and Nineveh. . .in the heart of Assyria. . .the lair of the bloodthirsty Baal and Astarte. . . .

And Abner? Sometime in the night he found himself, he did not know how, walking up the street the way he and Jonah had come earlier. But now there were no lanterns, no lights from any of the houses along the street. The street was flooded in light from a full moon. Abner came to the inn and turned to go in—and suddenly stopped. His heart skipped a beat.

There in front of him, on either side of the door, stood two men, still as statues. They were very tall and wore long white robes. Even in the moonlight their robes were dazzlingly bright. Abner could not quite see their faces, but somehow something seemed familiar about them. Where had he seen them? Suddenly he remembered. The two strange men sitting in that dark corner of the inn earlier tonight. He had not clearly seen their faces then either, only the outlines, and those robes, those powerful shoulders—yes, they looked the same. But why were they here now? They stood there, rigid, as though guarding the door to the inn. And somehow Abner had a feeling that, as long as these two men stood there, no one, or nothing, would ever get past them and into that inn.

He woke with a start and sat up in bed. Ah, it had been a dream, then. He lay down again. But now he was wide awake. The prophet in the other corner of the room stirred uneasily in his sleep. A pale light came in through the window. So there was a moon tonight, then. What about those two men? Abner wondered suddenly.

He pulled the blanket up to his chin and lay there, fighting the urge to go to the window and look down, to see if they were really there, by the door. It was only a dream, he told himself. Or was it? If they really were there, then what? Strangely, a peace seemed to settle over Abner. He remembered the feeling he had had as he stood there in the street watching the tall, silent figures in white by the door: All was well within that house!

I laid me down and slept; I awaked; for the LORD sustained me. I will not be afraid of ten thousands of people, that have set themselves against me round about.

PSALM 3:5–6

Abner lay there awhile, watching the silver moonlight in the window. The prophet had finally stopped tossing in his sleep and lay still now. His breathing had settled into an even rhythm.

And slowly, gently, Abner, too, slipped into deep, restful sleep.

Secret Code:

$\overline{}$ $\overline{}$ $\overline{}$ $\overline{}$
3-1-5-1 7-1-2-3 11-3-1-1 2-1-3-2

$\overline{}$ $\overline{}$ $\overline{}$ $\overline{}$
1-1-1-1 4-1-1-2 5-1-2-3 7-3-4-2

$\overline{}$ $\overline{}$ $\overline{}$ $\overline{}$ $\overline{}$
2-4-5-1 4-4-2-1 3-3-5-4 5-1-8-3 3-1-2-1

7
Jonah's True Love

It was six more days eastward to the ancient city of Mari, on the Euphrates River. It served as a garrison town guarding the river crossing. The caravan routes all intersected here—from Babylon, the Habor, and the Persian Gulf.

There was a temple to the Assyrian goddess Ishtar (Astarte) here. And there was another to the god Dagan. The entrance to this was guarded by two bronze lions with inlaid eyes. There were forty more such lions in this temple.

Jonah and Abner walked slowly past the ancient palace of Zimri-Lim. It covered a vast area, a small city in itself, with three hundred rooms. The walls of the massive throne room were covered by paintings. In the royal archives were some twenty thousand tablets, with laws and records dating back to the earliest history of the city.

Abner was staring in awe at the palace. Jonah was looking at the ground in front of his steps. Abner turned to Jonah to say something, but then stopped. Now was not the time for talk, the merchant could tell.

He had learned. On their journey through the desert, the prophet would often look like that—staring off into the distance as if in a trance. Sometimes when he was like that, there would be no word from him, not even a glance or a nod of his head, for hours, sometimes a day or more. At other times, though, he would seem to waken suddenly from a deep sleep, and then his eyes would be piercing and his voice sharp.

They went now along the street, Abner silent to respect the other's silence. The merchant found them an inn and, as was his habit, paid for their rooms and then unloaded his camel and carried his bundles up to his room. He always made sure his room had a lock and key. As Abner was doing this just now, the prophet stood

outside the door star-
ing down the street.

The innkeeper, a
fat, red-faced man, was
watching Jonah. As
Abner came down the
stairs, the innkeeper
asked him, "Some-
thing wrong with your
friend there?" jerking
his thumb toward Jonah.

"Oh, ah, I think a bit too much desert sun,"
Abner said.

The innkeeper looked warily at Jonah. "I do
not want any trouble here," he said, scowling.

"Oh, believe me, sir, we are no trouble. Just
two humble travelers who have come a long
way and who are in need of a good rest and
perhaps some good food and drink—which I
am sure can be had in abundance at this most
excellent establishment." He was smiling now
in his most appealing manner, rubbing his
hands together as if that food and drink were
already laid out before him.

"Hmmm," said the innkeeper.

Abner came up to him. He looked around
cautiously (there were only a few others in the

room, sitting quietly by themselves). Then he took out a little pouch and held it out to the innkeeper. There was a muffled metallic chink as the merchant dropped the little pouch into the innkeeper's hand.

"Now, ah, good sir, my friend and I are very hungry and thirsty and. . .and I think this"—pointing to the innkeeper's fat paw that had closed around the little pouch—"will be sufficient."

The innkeeper's face had lightened the moment he felt the pouch drop into his palm. His scowl was suddenly gone, replaced by a look that was almost kind. "Please, seat yourselves, sir, you and your worthy friend. There is indeed good food and drink here, as you shall see. Come, come!"

Abner bowed. "We are your servants," he said. Then he went out into the street and touched the prophet's arm.

Jonah did not move. Abner tapped him on the shoulder, steadily and gently, until the prophet finally blinked and gave a little shudder and then turned to look directly into the eyes of the merchant.

They went inside and sat down. Soon their table was laden with bowls of meat and baskets of rolls and a huge flagon of red wine.

As they ate, Abner stared at the table and said nothing. Now he was the one who appeared to be lost in his thoughts, or in some other place. The prophet looked at him and studied his face for awhile. Then Jonah did something he almost never did. He smiled. It did not come easily, though. It seemed to bend his features to its will, but only for a moment. Like a distant flare of light on a desert night, it flickered and then was gone.

But somehow the merchant had noticed. He blinked and turned to look at the prophet. The two men stared at each other for several moments.

Then Jonah said, very quietly, "Ask."

"Where were you this time? What'd you. . . see?"

And the prophet. . .what was this—another smile? No, not quite. But though the face did not change, the eyes, Abner thought, the eyes were smiling. "I saw nothing," Jonah said.

Abner looked stunned. "But. . .but. . . ," he said.

"And I heard nothing," Jonah added. "Not this time."

"Then what did you. . .where were you?"

"I do not always see anything," Jonah said. "And I hear something far less often."

"Then—then what do you. . .do?"

Jonah rested his chin on his fingers. "I watch," he said, quietly.

"Watch? But what do you watch, then?"

"I do not watch anything. I watch for something. For someone." He was not looking at Abner now, but was staring again, far, far away.

"For someone?"

"For the One I love. I watch for Him. I look for Him. For Him alone."

"The Lord? The Lord God?"

Jonah nodded. "Have you ever been in love?" he asked.

The little merchant's face changed. A sad, faraway look came over it. "Yes, I have," he said, almost in a whisper. "Once, long ago."

The prophet spoke tenderly now. "And your love for her made you blind to all others? You had eyes for her alone?"

Abner said nothing. His features were

marked with some deep pain.

"And all that mattered was to be with her," Jonah continued. "It mattered not whether she spoke or was silent. All was well with the world when you were by her side. A look from her, or a smile, was the source of all your joy. And a touch from her hand made your heart soar like the eagle."

Abner's voice was shaky. "Ah, you know of love, friend. There is nothing greater in all the world." A tear rolled down his cheek. "And there is no pain greater than love that is lost."

Jonah said, "I am sorry to have caused you pain, friend. But, you see, I am in love. The One I love is not of this earth. I do not see Him here." He gestured around him.

Abner looked at him curiously.

"Yes, I know, I ran from Him," the prophet said, "or tried to run. Do lovers never quarrel? Do they never disagree? I quarreled with the One I love. I was—I am afraid. But. . .but I love Him all the same."

The merchant nodded slowly. But then he looked troubled. "How is it that you—that the Lord—that I have never known Him like that?"

Jonah did not answer right away. He sat quietly for a few minutes. It appeared to Abner that the prophet was deep in thought.

Finally Jonah said, "Do you have many friends?"

"Aye, many!" Abner said, his face brightening a little.

"Yes, I think so. The world, I think, is your friend."

Abner spread out his arms as if in a wide embrace. "The world is my home," he said.

Jonah looked steadily into Abner's face for a moment. "It is not so for me. Nor has it ever been. I have few friends—few true friends. I have never found a place in this world to call my home, a place to lay my head. My place, my heart, is with the One who is not of this world."

"But does this One, the Lord, not love all men? Does He love some more than others?"

"Not some more than others. But it is one thing to be in love, and quite another thing to be loved in return. . .as you know."

A spasm of pain crossed Abner's face again. He looked down. "Ah, yes," he breathed.

"Am I in love with the Lord because this world hates me?" Jonah continued. "Or do I hate this world because I love the Lord? I do not know. I know only that He came like a lover to woo me, long ago. And like one whose heart can find no rest, I sought Him. He found me, and I found Him. My only desire now is to be with the One I love."

"And it is. . . with Him. . .where He speaks to you. . . shows you things?"

"It is. But it is not for His word, nor anything He chooses to show me, that I seek, that I watch for Him. I watch for Him."

> *My soul waiteth for the Lord more than they that watch for the morning: I say, more than they that watch for the morning.*
>
> PSALM 130:6

> *Behold, I stand at the door, and knock: if any man hear my voice, and open the door, I will come in to him, and will sup with him, and he with me.*
>
> REVELATION 3:20

Abner sat looking at his hands folded on the table. "How can I know the Lord like this, too?" he asked. "How can I be. . .in love with Him, too?"

Jonah looked into Abner's eyes. "Ask," he said. "Only ask. If it is your heart that asks—truly asks—He will answer."

Secret Code:

____ ____ ____
7-3-6-1 10-1-6-1 1-3-3-4

____ ____ ____ ____ ____ ____ ____.
4-1-1-1 8-5-5-1 9-2-1-2 2-2-5-4 3-2-1-1 5-2-6-1 6-1-4-6

8
Good Friends Part

It was their third morning in Mari. When Abner came downstairs into the main room of the inn, Jonah was there already, dressed in travel garb, his staff in his hand.

"It is time for me to go, friend," Jonah said.

"For you? For us, you mean?" said Abner, looking very worried.

"Not this time. The next part of my journey is into Assyria, as you know."

"Yes, but—but I have come so far. I have no intention of staying behind now."

Jonah looked at the little merchant kindly. "You are a good man. God will reward you for your generosity, and for your companionship, to me."

"God has rewarded me already. I know more of Him now than ever before. And I desire to know yet more."

"You will, my friend. You will indeed. But now I must finish my business. I go because I am sent. You have no business with the people to whom I go. It may be that they will have no business with you—or with me."

Abner stuck up his chin. "I am not afraid to die! I—I—not anymore, that is."

The prophet looked grave. "But to die by the hand of God is one kind of death. To die in vain is. . . . You do not really wish to die. That is vanity. I alone am sent to Nineveh. I will go—alone—to Nineveh." He put his hand on the other's shoulder. "I thank you, though, for all you have done for me. And I leave you with the blessing of the Lord. May your days be long and your ways prosperous, may your paths be safe and your direction sure." He looked hard into the merchant's face. "And as you seek, so may you find. May the Lord bring you to your heart's desire."

The two men embraced and then went out into the street. Abner held out a small pouch. "I cannot go with you," he said. "I think perhaps you are right. But this, my blessing, can go with you. You will need this. And I do not look for a reward—not in this life."

Jonah accepted the pouch and bowed. "Thank you, my friend, my brother. And who knows? If I return, I will reward you myself."

And they parted, Abner back into the inn, Jonah down the street to the east, to the crossing place on the river, toward Asshur, and toward Nineveh.

It was night on the desert. There was no moon. Overhead, the stars were spread like a vast canopy of black velvet covered with brilliant white diamonds. The hills lay huddled like drunken, sleeping giants. Against the misshapen bulk of these hills, a tiny bright flicker of orange seemed to be dancing.

A man sat before this dancing flicker, his campfire. He was draped in the white, flowing robe of a desert nomad.

He was four days into his journey. With some of the money the merchant had given him, he had bought a camel and a tent and other things he would need. The four days that had just passed could have been four years or four hours to the prophet. With no one to talk to him, to ask him questions, he did not have to keep his thoughts from wandering into other realms. The camel, he had been told by the trader in Mari, was a seasoned traveler. It would follow the caravan route across the desert no matter how far, no matter where it led.

This was fortunate for the man who walked beside the camel. He held the rope from the camel's halter and let the animal lead, on and on and on. And for these four days, every minute, every hour, the prophet had watched—not the road, not his steps, but that other place. . . and an image had been forming itself, taking shape out of the darkness of his thoughts.

He sat now watching his fire, but not seeing the fire. What did he see? A city. A city wall spread across the desert horizon. But only a ruin, empty and silent, the walls crumbled and fallen. . . .

[Nineveh] is empty, and void, and waste: and the heart melteth, and the knees smite together, and much pain is in all loins, and the faces of them all gather blackness.  *Where is the dwelling of the lions, and the feedingplace of the young lions, where the lion, even the old lion, walked, and the lion's whelp, and none made them afraid? The lion did tear in pieces enough for his whelps, and strangled for his lionesses, and filled his holes with prey, and his dens with ravin.*

NAHUM 2:10–12

75

The prophet's little fire was only a wisp now. He did not move, did not reach out to the pile of twigs and sticks to feed the dying fire. He did not even blink. The fire sputtered one last time and went out. The glowing embers slowly died away until all was darkness.

Complete darkness. . .no lights, anywhere, in the city. . .in that city. . . .

Woe to the bloody city! it is all full of lies and robbery; the prey departeth not; The noise of a whip, and the noise of the rattling of the wheels, and of the pransing horses, and of the jumping chariots. The horseman lifteth up both the bright sword and the glittering spear: and there is a multitude of slain, and a great number of carcases; and there is none end of their corpses; they stumble upon their corpses: Because of the multitude of the whoredoms of the wellfavoured harlot, the mistress of witchcrafts, that selleth nations through her whoredoms, and families through her witchcrafts. Behold, I am against thee, saith the LORD of hosts; and I will

discover thy skirts upon thy face, and
I will shew the nations thy nakedness,
and the kingdoms thy shame. And I
will cast abominable filth upon thee,
and make thee vile, and will set thee
as a gazingstock. And it shall come to
pass, that all they that look upon thee
shall flee from thee, and say, Nineveh
is laid waste: who will bemoan her?
whence shall I seek comforters for thee?

NAHUM 3:1–7

The desert night grew cold. The air was still. Somewhere in the distance a lion roared. Much closer, a hyena laughed. The camel, tethered by the side of the tent, lifted its head in alarm and snorted. The man sitting in front of the blackened, cold fire pit was as still as the rocks and hills of the desert. But it was too dark for anyone, if anyone had been there at that moment, to see whether the man's eyes were open or closed.

And [the LORD] will stretch out his
hand against the north, and destroy
Assyria; and will make Nineveh a
desolation, and dry like a wilderness.

And flocks shall lie down in the midst
of her, all the beasts of the nations:
both the cormorant and the bittern
shall lodge in the upper lintels of it;
their voice shall sing in the windows;
desolation shall be in the thresholds; for
he shall uncover the cedar work. This is
the rejoicing city that dwelt carelessly,
that said in her heart, I am, and there
is none beside me: how is she become
a desolation, a place for beasts to lie
down in! every one that passeth by her
shall hiss, and wag his hand.

ZEPHANIAH 2:13–15

Secret Code:

___	___	___
4-1-4-3	6-1-2-3	1-1-3-5

___	___	___
6-2-1-7	2-6-5-2	3-3-2-4

___	___	___	___	___
4-3-6-1	5-1-6-4	1-3-1-3	3-1-4-6	2-1-9-7

9
Nineveh at Last

The man stood in the dusty road holding the reins of his camel and staring in awe at what lay before him. It was still a long way off, but even from here it was imposing. Sweeping over the desert almost as far as the eye could see, it seemed at first sight to be an immense plateau rising up of itself out of the sand and rocks. But this plateau, Jonah had suddenly realized, was formed, not by God, but by the hand of man.

An empire within an empire was Nineveh. This was the resting place for the blood sorceress, the war goddess Ishtar—Astarte, the Queen of Heaven.

A sudden feeling of horror swept over Jonah. The hairs on the back of his neck prickled. Was this that dreaded place he had seen in the Spirit? But that place had been deserted, destroyed. Was this that city, in a time yet to come? When?

Go to Nineveh and preach against it. That was what the Lord had said. And, finally, Jonah was here.

He could feel the blood pulsing in his temples. His hand was shaking as it held the camel's halter. The prophet of God took a deep breath and started toward the city.

Nineveh was on a wide plain between the Tigris River to the east and the mountains to the west. The part of the river nearest the city was nearly four hundred feet wide. The wall that surrounded the entire city was one hundred feet high and wide enough on the top for three chariots to ride abreast. There were fifteen hundred towers, each two hundred feet tall, along this wall. The city was called a "three-days' journey"—it took three whole days to walk through it.

This was an old, old city. It was built by Nimrod the great hunter, the son of Cush, the son of Ham, the son of Noah. The corner of Nineveh facing the south and west was marked with a dedication to Nimrod, who was also called the world's first great conqueror.

And this was Nineveh, a city that thrived on conquest and bloodshed. Even so, it was not wholly evil. Although it was dedicated to Ishtar, the goddess of war, there was also a temple here for Nabu, the god of writing and arts and sciences. There were tens of thousands of texts in this huge temple. And within the city walls were great open spaces for cattle and sheep. More than half a million people made their home here.

But Nineveh worshipped evil gods. Her successive kings tried to outdo one another in cruelty to Nineveh's many victims—whole cities and nations. The blood of these victims, over the centuries, cried out to God for vengeance.

And today, God's judgment came to

Nineveh. His voice, the one He sent as messenger, was within its walls.

Jonah was walking slowly up the street. This time, though, he did not go as one distracted, as one in a dream. His features were set as in stone, and his eyes burned with a blue fire. Something about the way he carried himself, about his face—the people teeming about in the street, every one of them, it seemed, saw him coming, made room for him, and stood staring open-mouthed at his back as he passed.

He stopped before a man in a white robe with the insignia of an official on his shoulder. The man opened his mouth to speak, but then suddenly stood frozen, his mouth gaping.

"Tell everyone," Jonah said—that voice!—

"that the servant of the Living God, the God of Israel and Judah, is here." The official felt as though his knees suddenly turned to water. "Tell everyone that this God, the one true God, commanded me, His servant, to come to you to warn you of your doom. I disobeyed his command, and I went to the bottom of the sea in the belly of a fish for three days. Then God commanded me again, and I obeyed. My life is now a sign to you, to all of Nineveh."

Jonah held up three fingers. "Three days I was within the jaws of death. Then I was restored to life. I am here now, and I bring the word of God to you. Now go, tell everyone to tell everyone—every one!"

In all the streets, in all the houses, in the shops, in the marketplaces, everyone was telling everyone to tell everyone—a stranger was in the city. . .a servant of the God of Israel. . .a messenger. . .sent by God to speak to Nineveh. . . disobeyed. . .three days in. . .in the what?. . . yes, that's right, the belly of a fish. . .delivered from that place of death. . . sent again. . .was here now, in the very street. . . .

"In forty days Nineveh will be destroyed!" The voice rang out over the clamor of the busy street. Heads turned; mouths stopped.

"There!" came the sharp whispers.

"That man!"

"He's the one."

"The one who—?"

"Yes, yes! In the belly of a fish. Three days!"

"You don't believe it, do you?"

"I don't know, I—do you?"

The man cried out again:

"In forty days Nineveh will be destroyed!"

It was not just the man. It was not just the words he shouted. It was not even the story he had told. It was the anointing. The power of God was the force that sent the words into the hearts of all who heard, that seemed to turn their very bones to butter.

All along the street now, ashen faces were fixed on the man shouting in the street; eyes were wide in terror; mouths were open but silent. Ahead of Jonah, farther and farther into the city, the news was spreading like a fire over a dry grassland. All of Nineveh, it seemed, was out on that street today. There were the merely curious, the scornful, the unbelieving—that was the way they came.

But then when they heard for themselves. . .

"In forty days Nineveh will be destroyed!"

. . .Nineveh, from the youngest to the oldest—believed.

So the people of Nineveh believed
God, and proclaimed a fast, and put
on sackcloth, from the greatest of
them even to the least of them. For
word came unto the king of Nineveh,
and he arose from his throne, and he
laid his robe from him, and covered
him with sackcloth, and sat in ashes.
And he caused it to be proclaimed
and published through Nineveh by
the decree of the king and his nobles,
saying, Let neither man nor beast, herd
nor flock, taste any thing: let them not
feed, nor drink water: But let man and
beast be covered with sackcloth, and
cry mightily unto God: yea, let them
turn every one from his evil way, and
from the violence that is in their hands.
Who can tell if God will turn and
repent, and turn away from his fierce
anger, that we perish not?

JONAH 3:5–9

Jonah had gone to the end of the city, three days of walking. On his way back, the streets were deserted, the city strangely quiet. The people he did see, half hidden in shadows between buildings and through doorways, stared at him in silence. Many of them wore sackcloth, their faces smeared with ashes.

He went up now out of Nineveh toward the mountains to the east. He climbed up into the foothills and made a hasty shelter out of branches. He sat down to wait, and to watch.

And he was bitter.

And he prayed unto the LORD, and said, I pray thee, O LORD, was not this my saying, when I was yet in my country? Therefore I fled before unto Tarshish: for I knew that thou art a gracious God, and merciful, slow to anger, and of great kindness, and repentest thee of the evil. Therefore now, O LORD, take, I beseech thee, my life from me; for it is better for me to die than to live.

Then said the LORD, Doest thou well to be angry?

JONAH 4:2–4

Jonah did not answer. He sat there, watching the city below him, nursing his bitterness.

"My worst fear, then," he said to himself, "is come true! I was ready to die then, and I am ready to die now, rather than use the name of the Lord—and His word—in vain. The heathen will say—and then Israel, too, will say—'The word of the Lord God is not a solid foundation.' They will say, 'The Lord God is not to be trusted. He cannot make up His mind! Who can believe what He says?' So they will say, even my own people. And all this will be because of me!"

Jonah was very tired. Beyond the city toward the west, the sun was going down over the river. Jonah lay down and slept.

When he woke he was startled to see that a green plant had grown up overnight. Already it was the size of a small olive tree. Jonah recognized the plant, the palmcrist. It had broad, flat leaves, like those of a vine. It was very pleasant in the cool shade of this tree.

Jonah was exceeding glad of the gourd.

But God prepared a worm when the morning rose the next day, and it smote the gourd that it withered.

And it came to pass, when the sun did arise, that God prepared a vehement east wind; and the sun beat upon the head of Jonah, that he fainted, and wished in himself to die, and said, It is better for me to die than to live.

And God said to Jonah, Doest thou well to be angry for the gourd? And he said, I do well to be angry, even unto death.

Then said the LORD, Thou hast had pity on the gourd, for the which thou hast not laboured, neither madest it grow; which came up in a night, and perished in a night: And should not I spare Nineveh, that great city, wherein are more than sixscore thousand

*persons that cannot discern between
their right hand and their left hand;
and also much cattle?*

JONAH 4:6–11

Secret Code:

<u>   </u>   <u>   </u>
3-2-2-3 5-1-5-7

<u>   </u>   <u>   </u>   <u>   </u>   <u>   </u>   <u>   </u>
2-2-3-7 4-2-3-5 1-1-1-3 3-2-1-1 6-1-1-1

<u>   </u>   <u>   </u>   <u>   </u>   <u>   </u>   <u>   </u>
9-3-1-4 2-4-5-1 3-1-4-1 6-9-4-5 7-1-4-6

10
Jonah Learns of God's Mercy

"So you are still here, I see."

The little merchant looked up suddenly. A stranger stood in the open doorway, his back to the late-morning sun. The merchant, shading his eyes and blinking into the sunlight, could not make out the face. But the voice! Surely he knew that voice.

"Jonah!"

The man walked into the inn. And for only the second time since Abner had known him, the prophet smiled.

The merchant jumped up from his table

and embraced his friend. "The Lord God be praised!" he said. "I truly wondered if I would ever see you again."

To the innkeeper Abner shouted, "Please, some breakfast for my friend." Then to Jonah he said, "Please sit down with me and be my guest. And when you wish, tell me of your, ah, your journey."

"My destination, you mean? For, yes, my journey had an end."

"And—well, ah, may I ask, what was the end?"

"Salvation."

Abner gasped. "For. . .for. . .Nineveh?"

Jonah nodded. "Repentance," he said. "Repentance and. . .they are saved."

Abner was just staring at the prophet's face. He could say nothing.

"And I?" said Jo-
nah. "Well may you ask, what of me?" He shrugged. "What can I say? In my passion to uphold the Lord's good name, His word, I chose even death rather than obedience. Yet I did

not know the one to whom I owe my life—nay, my resurrected life—as well as I had thought."

"You? But you—you are His, His—"

"Yes, I am His friend, as well as His servant. But I am ashamed to tell you that I, even I, did not know His heart so well as I should have—so well as, I think, I do now. He is a God of mercy, far more than He is a God of wrath."

"Ah," breathed Abner. He folded his hands on the table and bowed his head. "Ah, a God of mercy! Amen." His eyes were closed. A tear rolled down his cheek.

In another place, in another time, many, many years after the prophet called Jonah, a group of men stood before one whom they called Teacher. (Others called him the Christ, the Promised One, the Son of God.)

> *Then certain of the scribes and of the Pharisees answered, saying, Master, we would see a sign from thee.*
> *But he answered and said unto them, An evil and adulterous generation seeketh after a sign; and there shall no sign be given to it, but the sign of the prophet Jonas: For as Jonas*

was three days and three nights in the whale's belly; so shall the Son of man be three days and three nights in the heart of the earth. The men of Nineveh shall rise in judgment with this generation, and shall condemn it: because they repented at the preaching of Jonas; and, behold, a greater than Jonas is here.

MATTHEW 12:38–41

"Greater than Jonah" indeed! Jonah brought salvation to the Ninevites because he obeyed God and preached to them. Jesus Christ is the One who is preached! Jonah spoke the word of God. Jesus is the Word of God!

In the beginning was the Word, and the Word was with God, and the Word was God. The same was in the beginning with God. All things were made by him; and without him was not any thing made that was made. In him was life; and the life was the light of men. And the light shineth in darkness; and the darkness comprehended it not.

JOHN 1:1–5

And the Word was made flesh, and dwelt among us, (and we beheld his glory, the glory as of the only begotten of the Father,) full of grace and truth.

JOHN 1:14

The sign of Jonah (his "death" in the belly of the fish for three days, and then his "resurrection") was to Nineveh. This sign, and the word that God spoke to Nineveh through Jonah, brought repentance and salvation to the Ninevites (even though their repentance, and salvation, was only temporary).

This sign was a type, a prophecy, of the death and resurrection of the Lord Jesus Christ. Through His death (and He was buried three days) and resurrection, the "Word (that) was made flesh and dwelt

among us" became salvation to all who believe in Him. And this salvation is eternal!

And as Moses lifted up the serpent in the wilderness, even so must the

Son of man be lifted up: That whosoever believeth in him should not perish, but have eternal life.

For God so loved the world, that he gave his only begotten Son, that whosoever believeth in him should not perish, but have everlasting life.

JOHN 3:14–16

That if thou shalt confess with thy mouth the Lord Jesus, and shalt believe in thine heart that God hath raised him from the dead, thou shalt be saved. For with the heart man believeth unto righteousness; and with the mouth confession is made unto salvation.

For the scripture saith, Whosoever believeth on him shall not be ashamed.

For there is no difference between the Jew and the Greek: for the same Lord over all is rich unto all that call upon him. For whosoever shall call upon the name of the Lord shall be saved.

ROMANS 10:9–13

Secret Code:

$\overline{\text{3-3-2-5}}$ $\overline{\text{1-2-3-5}}$ $\overline{\text{4-1-4-4}}$

$\overline{\text{1-4-5-2}}$ $\overline{\text{2-6-3-4}}$ $\overline{\text{3-2-3-1}}$ $\overline{\text{2-4-1-4}}$ $\overline{\text{3-1-5-3}}$ $\overline{\text{2-1-3-3}}$ $\overline{\text{1-1-1-1}}$.